Hello Kitty's SUPER-DUPER VALENTINE'S DAY PARTY

By Kris Hirschmann
Illustrated by Sachiho Hino

SCHOLASTIC INC.
New York   Toronto   London   Auckland   Sydney
Mexico City   New Delhi   Hong Kong   Buenos Aires

Decorate all of the pictures in this book with stickers. The page numbers on the sticker page will help you figure out which stickers to use.

ISBN 0-439-81309-3

12 11 10 9 8 7 6 5 4 3 2 1   6 7 8 9 10 11/0

Printed in the U.S.A.
First printing, January 2006

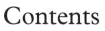

Contents

Chapter 1
You're Invited

One sunny winter morning, Hello Kitty was eating her favorite breakfast. Her sister, Mimmy, was sitting next to her at the table. Papa was rocking in his chair and reading the newspaper. Mama was standing at the stove making pancakes.

"It's the first day of February, girls," Mama said. "Who wants to change the calendar?"

"Me!" cried Hello Kitty. She

walked over to the calendar. She lifted the bottom page.

"*Ohhhh!*" she and Mimmy said together. "How pretty!" The calendar had pictures of tiny hearts on it. There was another heart on the space for February 14. Hello  Kitty knew what the hearts meant. Valentine's Day was almost here!

"Can I have a Valentine's Day party, Mama?" she asked. "Please?"

"That would be fun!" said Mama. "Of course you can."

Valentine's Day was less than two weeks away. Hello Kitty knew she had to make invitations right now! She got out colored paper and scissors. She folded the pieces of paper in half.

Then she cut the paper like this:

Hello Kitty unfolded the pieces of paper. Each one was shaped like a heart. So far, so good!

She decorated the paper hearts with stickers, lace, and glitter.

Hello Kitty couldn't wait to get to school and hand out her pretty invitations. It was going to be the best party ever!

Please come to my
Super-Duper
Valentine's Day Party!

February 14
4 PM
See you there!
Love, Hello Kitty

Hello Kitty's

Super-Duper Party Diary

Mama said I could have a Valentine's Day party. I can't wait! I'm going to invite everyone I know.

Chapter 2
A Bad Fall

At lunch the next day, Hello Kitty told her friends about her party.

"Will there be games?" asked Fifi.

"Of course!" said Hello Kitty.

"And food?" asked Joey.

"There will be delicious food," said Hello Kitty. "And balloons and streamers and music and dancing, too."

"Hooray!" everyone said. "Your party sounds super, Hello Kitty."

Just then the bell
rang. It was time to
go back to class.
Hello Kitty and her

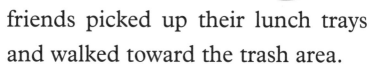

friends picked up their lunch trays
and walked toward the trash area.

Hello Kitty was thinking so much
about her party that she forgot to
look where she was going. She didn't
see the puddle of milk on the floor.
Hello Kitty stepped right in it!

WHOOPS! Her feet flew out from
under her. She fell to the floor with a
loud THUMP. Her lunch tray crashed
down nearby.

"Oh, no!" cried Kathy and Tippy.
They rushed to their friend's side.

They helped Hello Kitty stand up.

"OUCH!" cried Hello Kitty when her right foot touched the ground. "Ooooh, my ankle! It hurts!" A big tear rolled down Hello Kitty's cheek.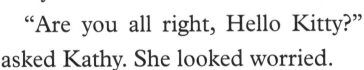

"Are you all right, Hello Kitty?" asked Kathy. She looked worried.

"I don't think so," Hello Kitty sniffed. "I think I need to see the doctor."

February

Sun.	Mon.	Tue.	Wed.	Thu.	Fri.	Sat.
1	2	3	4	5	6	7
8	9	10	11	12	13	14
15	16	17	18	19	20	21
22	23	24	25	26	27	28

Chapter 3
At the Doctor's Office

Mama and Papa took Hello Kitty to the doctor. She sat on the table with her leg sticking out in front of her. Her ankle was too sore to touch.

A nurse had taken an X-ray of Hello Kitty's foot.

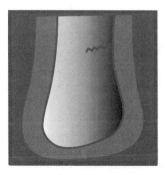

Now the doctor was looking at the X-ray. "You have a fracture. That's a little crack in your ankle bone. I want to put a cast on it. You must stay off your feet for a couple of weeks."

Hello Kitty thought about her Valentine's Day party. It was less than two weeks away! Hello Kitty was going to have to cancel her party. This was a disaster!

FROM THE DOCTOR'S DESK

Hello Kitty:
Rest your leg for
at least two weeks.
No walking unless you
absolutely have to!

Hello Kitty's Super-Duper Party Diary
I can't believe I have to
cancel my party. Why did I
have to hurt my ankle?
It's just not fair!

Chapter 4
Mimmy's Great Idea

That evening, Hello Kitty lay on her bed at home. Kathy, Tippy, Joey, Fifi, and Mimmy stood around the bed. They had brought flowers and a get-well card for their friend. The room looked pretty, but everyone was glum.

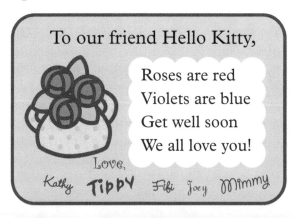

To our friend Hello Kitty,

Roses are red
Violets are blue
Get well soon
We all love you!

Love,
Kathy Tippy Fifi Joey Mimmy

"I'm sorry you hurt yourself, Hello Kitty," said Fifi. "And I'm so sorry your party is canceled, too. We were all looking forward to it."

"I know," said Hello Kitty sadly. She wanted to cry every time she thought about it.

Suddenly, Mimmy had an idea. "Maybe we can still have the party," she said slowly.

"No, Mimmy. I'm not allowed to walk. I can't do it," said Hello Kitty.

"*You* don't have to do anything, Hello Kitty," said Mimmy. "We can do it for you! Can't we?" She looked around the room hopefully.

Everyone started to smile. "I can be in charge of games," said Fifi.

"I'll buy the food," said Joey.

"I want to get the balloons and streamers!" said Tippy.

"I'll choose the music," said Kathy.

"And I'll order the cake," finished Mimmy. "Hello Kitty, you can be the guest of honor."

"You would really do that for me?" asked Hello Kitty.

"Of course," Joey replied. "That's what friends are for." Everyone nodded.

"Plus, it will be fun," added Mimmy. "We are going to throw the best Valentine's Day party ever. Just wait and see!"

Super-Duper Party Diary
The party is on again!
I have the best friends
in the world.

Chapter 5
The Big Day Arrives

February 14 finally came. All over town, Hello Kitty's friends woke up bright and early. There was a lot of work to do before party time.

Papa took Mimmy, Fifi, Joey, Tippy, and Kathy to the supermarket. Fifi headed to the toy aisle to look for games. Joey zipped over to the food section. Tippy went to the party aisle, and Kathy walked through the music aisle. Soon everyone

had what they needed.

Mimmy went to the bakery. She had ordered the perfect cake, and she couldn't wait to pick it up.

Hello Kitty watched Papa and Mimmy leave the house. She felt sad. She was glad the party wasn't canceled, but she was feeling left out.

Then Hello Kitty had a thought. A Valentine's Day party needed valentines—and she knew how to make the cutest cards ever!

With Mama's help, Hello Kitty sat at her craft table. First she cut square cards out of colorful paper. On each card, she wrote a special Valentine's Day message. Then she made heart-shaped envelopes for the cards and tucked each one into an envelope.

To: Kathy
Happy
Valentine's
Day!

Hello Kitty was pleased with herself.

She smiled when she was finished. *Now I can give everyone a little surprise,* she thought.

Super-Duper Party Diary

I made the cutest valentines today. They're bright pink and red. I hope everyone at the party likes them!

Chapter 6
The Perfect Cake

The morning passed quickly. It was almost party time! Everyone went to Hello Kitty's house to get ready. They brought all the supplies they had bought earlier that day.

Soon everyone was busy. Fifi taped a big poster to the wall for a pin-the-heart-on-the-teddy-bear game. Tippy put balloons and streamers all around the room. Kathy piled a big stack of CDs on a table.

Joey set the table for a *Valentine's Day* feast.

Hello Kitty sat in a chair. *I wish I was working, too!* she thought as she watched her busy friends. *But everything looks wonderful. I guess they don't need my help to throw a super-duper party.* Just then there was a noise at the doorway. Everyone turned to look. It was Mimmy with the biggest, prettiest, pink-and-red-and-white *Valentine's Day* cake ever.

"*Oooooh!*" cried everyone. "It's beautiful!

Mimmy smiled proudly. She carried the cake toward the table. As she was setting it down, the platter tilted. The cake started to slide!

"Mimmy! The cake is *slipping!*" cried Fifi and Kathy.

Mimmy gasped. She tried to hold the platter level. But it was too late. CRASH! The big, pretty, pink-and-red-and-white cake fell to the floor and broke into a hundred pieces!

Hello Kitty's

Super-Duper Party Diary
Mimmy's cake was so pretty. It's so sad that it fell on the floor! I wish I could have done something to help!

Chapter 7
Mama to the Rescue

"Oh, no!" wailed Mimmy. "Our beautiful cake! I ruined it!"

Kathy gave Mimmy a hug. "Don't feel bad," she said. "Our party will be fun even without a cake."

"But it won't be perfect," Mimmy said sadly.

Hello Kitty just watched and listened. Poor Mimmy! Hello Kitty wished she could do something to make her sister feel better.

Then she had an idea. "Tippy, will you take me to the kitchen?" she asked.

"Of course," he said. He helped Hello Kitty stand up. Hello Kitty put her arm around Tippy's shoulders. She carefully hopped to the kitchen on her good leg. Tippy helped Hello Kitty sit at the table.

Mama was standing at the sink. "Mama, do you know how to bake a heart-shaped cake?" said Hello Kitty.

"Yes, I do," said Mama.

Mama mixed up a big batch of cake batter. She poured half of the batter into a round pan. She poured the other half into a square pan. Then she popped both pans into the oven to bake.

When the cakes were done, Mama took them out of the oven. She cut the round cake in half. Then she arranged the cakes on a platter like this:

Mama put the platter on the table. She gave Hello Kitty cups with colored frosting in them. She handed Hello Kitty a plastic knife.

"You can decorate the cake," she said.

"Thank you, Mama!" said Hello Kitty. She was thrilled. **FINALLY,** there was something she could do to help!

Make and decorate your
own heart-shaped cake.
See the instructions on page 46.

Super-Duper Party Diary

Mama showed me how
to make the most beautiful
cake today. Mama knows
everything. She is the best
mother in the world!

Chapter 8
A Super-Duper Party

At four o' clock, the party started.

"Wow!" Hello Kitty's friends said when they opened the playroom door. "The room looks great!"

Balloons, streamers, and hearts were everywhere. Fun games sat in one corner. A big dancing area had been cleared right in the middle of the room.

But the dinner table was the best part of all. On it sat a beautiful, heart-shaped pink-and-red-and white cake.

"That's the nicest Valentine's Day cake I've ever seen," said Tracy.

"Yes! Thank you, Hello Kitty!" everyone said.

Hello Kitty beamed with joy. "I'm so glad you like it," she said. "But you don't need to thank me. I should be thanking you. We wouldn't be having a party at all if Mimmy, Kathy, Fifi, Tippy, and Joey hadn't worked so hard. I have a surprise for everyone."

Hello Kitty handed out all the

valentines she had made.

"How sweet, Hello Kitty!" cried her friends.

"We have a surprise, too," said Joey. He opened a box full of crayons, markers, and other craft supplies. Everyone grabbed something from the box.

"What are you doing?" asked Hello Kitty.

"We're going to make your cast into a valentine," answered Joey.

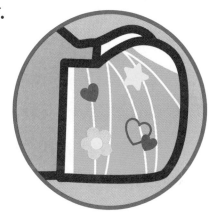

Everyone helped to decorate Hello Kitty's cast. Soon it was covered with hearts, flowers, rainbows, and messages.

"Now you *can't* forget how much we love you," said Mimmy.

Hello Kitty was so happy. "You are the best friends I could ever have!" she said. "Now it's time to have fun."

Everyone did just that. They played games and ate food and listened to music and danced.

Hello Kitty watched. But, she didn't feel left out. She just felt glad that everyone was having such a good time.

I may have hurt my ankle, she thought, *but that didn't stop me— and my friends—from having the superest-duperest* Valentine's Day party *ever!*

Hello Kitty's Valentines

Make valentines in heart-shaped envelopes, just like Hello Kitty!

You will need:
Colored paper
Scissors
Pencil
Glue stick

Crayons, markers, glitter, lace, or anything else for decorating.

What you do:

1. Find the square inside the shape on page 45. Trace it onto a piece of colored paper. Cut out the square.

2. Write your Valentine's Day message on it. Then decorate it any way you like.

3. To make the envelope, trace the entire shape onto another piece of colored paper. Cut it out.

4. Fold up one bottom flap. Put a little bit of glue on the edge of the flap.

5. Fold up the other bottom flap. Press to glue the flaps together. Wait until they dry.

6. Decorate the envelope. Put the note inside and give it to a friend!

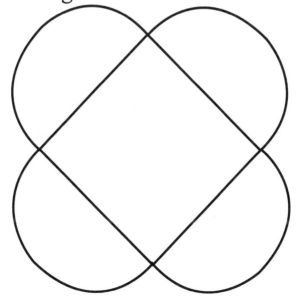

Mama's Heart-Shaped Cake

Valentine cakes are easy to make. Just ask a grown-up to help you bake.

You will need:
A box of cake mix
Round 8-inch (20-cm) cake pan
Square 8-inch (20-cm) cake pan
White frosting
Food coloring
Platter
Plastic cups
Plastic knife

What you do:

1. Ask a grown-up to mix the cake batter for you and prepare the pans. Follow the instructions on the cake box.

2. Pour half of the batter into the round pan. Pour the other half into the square pan.

3. Follow the instructions on the cake box to bake the cakes!

4. When the cakes are done, have a grown-up take them out of the oven. Let them cool.

5. Take the cakes out of the pans and put them on a platter. Ask a grown-up to cut the round cake in half.

6. Arrange the cakes just like Mama did on page 35. Put a little bit of frosting where the edges of the cakes meet. This will "glue" the cakes together.

7. Put white frosting into a few different cups. Use food coloring to color the frosting.

8. Decorate your cake any way you like!

Chapter 5 — page 23

Chapter 6 — page 26

Chapter 7 — page 36

Chapter 8 — page 38

ISBN: S-T29-81309-3